# The Flying Chinese Wonders

**CATCH ALL OF FLAT STANLEY'S WORLDWIDE ADVENTURES:**

The Mount Rushmore Calamity

The Great Egyptian Grave Robbery

The Japanese Ninja Surprise

The Intrepid Canadian Expedition

The Amazing Mexican Secret

The African Safari Discovery

The Flying Chinese Wonders

**AND DON'T MISS ANY OF THESE OUTRAGEOUS STORIES:**

Flat Stanley: His Original Adventure!

Stanley and the Magic Lamp

Invisible Stanley

Stanley's Christmas Adventure

Stanley in Space

Stanley, Flat Again!

# FLAT STANLEY's
## WORLDWIDE ADVENTURES
### BOOK NO. 7

## The Flying Chinese
# Wonders

CREATED BY **Jeff Brown**
WRITTEN BY **Josh Greenhut**
PICTURES BY **Macky Pamintuan**

**HARPER**
*An Imprint of HarperCollinsPublishers*

Library of Congress Cataloging-in-Publication Data
Greenhut, Josh.
    The Flying Chinese Wonders / created by Jeff Brown ; written by Josh
Greenhut ; pictures by Macky Pamintuan.—1st ed.
        p.    cm.— (Flat Stanley's worldwide adventures ; 7)
    Summary: When he inadvertently injures a Chinese acrobat performing at
his school auditorium, Stanley travels with the brother and sister duo to Beijing
where he trains to perform for the president of China.
    ISBN 978-0-06-143003-9 (trade bdg.)— ISBN 978-0-06-143002-2 (pbk. bdg.)
    [1. Acrobatics—Fiction. 2. Adventure and adventurers—Fiction.
3. China—Fiction.] I. Brown, Jeff, 1926–2003. II. Pamintuan, Macky, ill.
III. Title.
PZ7.G84568Fl  2011                                          2010022977
[Fic]—dc22                                                          CIP
                                                                    AC
Typography by Alison Klapthor
        12  13  14  15    LP/RRDC    10 9 8 7 6 5 4 3 2
❖
First Edition

# CONTENTS

# Unlucky Day

The fact that Stanley Lambchop was flat did not mean he enjoyed being treated like a poster.

Stanley trudged back and forth outside the school auditorium with two giant pieces of cardboard covering the front and back of his body. Both sides read:

## THE FLYING CHINESE WONDERS!
## A CHINESE NEW YEAR PERFORMANCE
## FOR THE WHOLE COMMUNITY

People streamed inside. A beefy boy from Stanley's class called out, "Look, it's the poster boy for flat kids!"

Stanley grimaced. He hoped no one else would notice him.

"Well, hello there, Stanley Lambchop!" It was Doctor Dan, whom Stanley had visited just after he was flattened. It wasn't long ago that he'd woken up to find that his bulletin board had fallen on him in the middle of the night. "Helping out with the big performance, are we? Well, good for you for making positive use of an unusual condition!"

How embarrassing, Stanley thought.

After Doctor Dan left to take his seat, Stanley's family appeared. "My little star!" squealed his mother, Harriet Lambchop.

Stanley tried to smile as she kissed the edge of his head.

His little brother, Arthur, rolled his eyes. "He's not even *in the show,* Mom."

"Now, Arthur," Mrs. Lambchop said, "those behind the scenes are just as important as those onstage."

"And nobody is behind the scenes like our Stanley." Mr. Lambchop winked. Stanley sighed. He'd always liked being in plays. Now, all anyone wanted him to do was move the sets, because his shape made him hard to see when he crossed the stage.

"I'm not even moving scenery today," Stanley grumbled.

"Why not?" asked Mr. Lambchop.

"Are you in charge of the giant pandas?" said Mrs. Lambchop hopefully. "They have always been my favorite wonders from China!"

"No." Stanley pouted. "There aren't any pandas. The spotlight blew a fuse, so . . ." He held up a giant flashlight from behind his poster. "I have to hang upside down from the ceiling with this."

"Hey, Stanley," called his friend

Carlos, who lived next door to the Lambchops. "Don't break a leg!"

Stanley's mother chuckled. "He means, 'Break a leg,' dear. That's a common figure of speech in the theater. It means good luck!" Harriet Lambchop took great interest in the proper use of the English language.

"I don't think so, Mom," said Arthur. "I think Carlos meant, 'Don't fall from the ceiling and break your leg.'"

"Be quiet, Arthur," huffed Stanley.

Once everyone was seated, Stanley took his place. He hung with his lower body rolled around a bar high over the crowd.

It's not fair! he thought. Why do I have to save the day any time somebody needs something flat or flexible?

On the one hand, Stanley's new shape allowed him to do lots of fun and exciting things, like fit between the walls of an Egyptian pyramid and be a cape in a Mexican bullfight. On the other hand, he was often asked to do uncomfortable, humiliating, and boring things that would never be expected of a rounded person. For instance, he was rolled and tied to the back of a horse in South Dakota and forced to ride with baggage in the cargo hold of an airplane to Africa.

Stanley didn't want to hang high

in the air holding a heavy flashlight. He didn't even know what to expect onstage. The performers had arrived only moments before the show was about to begin.

The lights went down. With a sigh, Stanley lifted his flashlight and flicked it on as the curtains squeaked open.

In the center of the bare stage stood

a teenage boy and girl. They wore matching red outfits.

"Lucky people of America!" A Chinese man in a tuxedo stepped onto the stage. "All the way from the People's Republic of China, we bring to you . . . the Flying Chinese Wonders!"

A few people clapped as Stanley moved like a spotlight back and forth between the two performers. They bowed slowly.

This is going to be even worse than I thought, figured Stanley.

Then, in a flash, the boy and girl shot into the air. Flipping high over the stage, they grabbed hands and flattened their bodies, spinning around

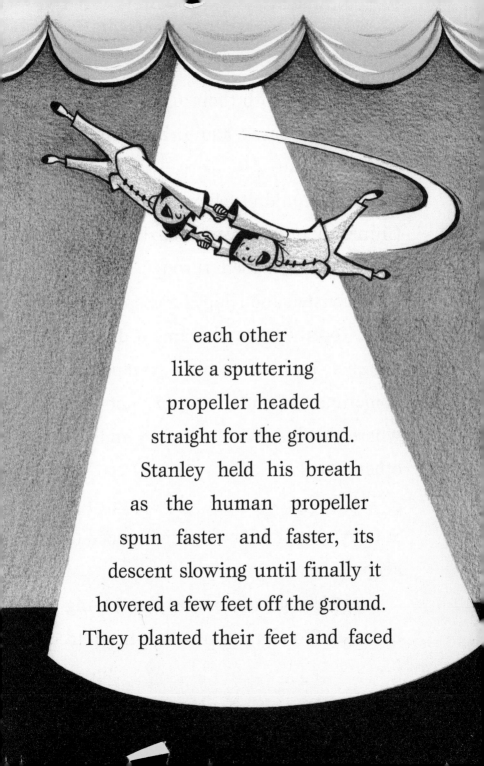

each other
like a sputtering
propeller headed
straight for the ground.
Stanley held his breath
as the human propeller
spun faster and faster, its
descent slowing until finally it
hovered a few feet off the ground.
They planted their feet and faced

the audience with their arms raised in the air. The entire auditorium erupted with applause.

Stanley couldn't believe it! The Flying Chinese Wonders were amazing! They swooped and sailed through the air. They twisted and flipped and spun like tops. Together, they became a dragon, a comet, and a fish on a trampoline. Sometimes, Stanley could not tell where the first Wonder began and the other ended.

Their bodies can do anything! Stanley thought. His flashlight raced to keep up.

For their grand finale, the Flying Chinese Wonders connected head to toe, puffed out their chests to form a circle, and rolled around the stage. When they came to a stop, each held out an arm and a leg. The giant circle had become the sun.

It was the greatest thing Stanley had ever seen! He shouted, whooped, and clapped his—

Stanley's heart plummeted as he watched the giant flashlight drop from his hands.

CRAAASH!

The Flying Chinese Wonders looked up in alarm. Their circle shook . . . and collapsed to the floor in a heap.

# "Knee How"

Stanley led Doctor Dan to the dressing room backstage. The girl acrobat opened the door, and Doctor Dan rushed in and bent over the boy acrobat, who was stretched out on a table.

Stanley tried to make himself invisible by pressing himself against the wall. It didn't work.

The girl Chinese Wonder studied

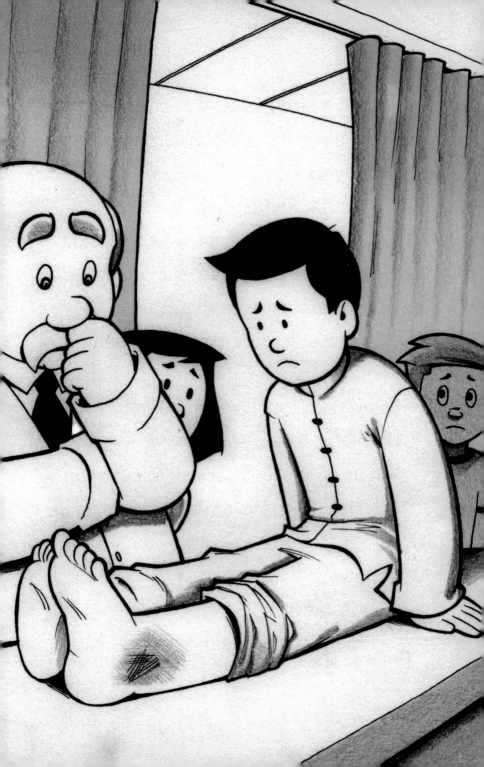

Stanley's face.

"You are like art," she marveled, "yet your eyes move!"

"I'm flat," whispered Stanley.

The girl looked impressed. "I would like to be flat! I am Yin," she continued. "That is my twin brother, Yang."

"I'm Stanley and I'm sorry!" blurted Stanley. "I was hanging from the ceiling being the spotlight and I dropped the flashlight!"

The girl's eyes widened. Yang sat up from the table. He blinked.

"Yin, do you see a turnip cake shaped like a boy?"

"Yes, brother."

"Good," Yang said and lay back

down. "I thought the pain was tricking my mind."

Doctor Dan cleared his throat. "Young man, I'm afraid you have a broken foot."

"No!" Yin gasped.

"Impossible," said Yang, sitting up again. "The Flying Chinese Wonders have never been injured."

"I'm sorry," said Doctor Dan. "If it makes you feel better, Stanley here had never been flat before. But then one day he visited me and he was only half an inch thick. Your foot will take at least six weeks to heal."

Yin's eyes welled with tears. "Doctor . . ." She gulped. "We are to perform in Beijing for the culmination of the Chinese New Year festivities in two weeks! It is to be our biggest and most important performance ever!"

"I'm sorry," said Doctor Dan. "I know it's disappointing, but you'll have to cancel. I'd better go get a splint for this foot."

After Doctor Dan left, Yin went over to her brother, took his hand, and kneeled beside him. Neither of them looked at Stanley.

"This is all my fault," Stanley said quietly. Then he folded himself to the ground and buried his face in his knees.

After a moment, Yang spoke. "Confucius said, 'Our greatest glory is not in never failing, but in getting up every time we do.' Get up, sister. Get up, Turnip Cake. The Flying Chinese Wonders have never missed a performance, and they will not now."

"But how, brother?" said Yin. "How can you perform with a broken foot?"

"I will not," Yang said solemnly. "Turnip Cake will."

"But, brother—!"

"I'm not an acrobat," said Stanley.

"Are you flexible?" said Yang.

Stanley shrugged. "I once went down Niagara Falls wrapped around somebody like a barrel," he offered.

"Are you strong?"

"I did keep Abraham Lincoln's nose from breaking off Mount Rushmore."

"Are you determined?"

"I recently walked halfway across Mexico to get a recipe for my mom," said Stanley.

"Then you will learn," said Yang.

Stanley looked at Yin. She nodded in approval.

Stanley imagined himself standing atop the Great Wall of China, and a smile spread across his face.

"I'll do my best," he promised.

Four days later, Stanley was sorted and loaded for special delivery deep in the

Shaanxi province of China. He could feel the wheels of a bicycle carrying his envelope along a craggy road.

Eventually, the wheels came to a stop, and Stanley's envelope was torn open. Yin's face peeked inside.

"Hello, Stanley," she said with a grin. "Welcome to China!"

"Knee how!" cried Stanley. He hopped out and stretched his legs.

"You hurt your knee?" she said in a panic.

"Knee how," repeated Stanley. "Isn't that how you say 'hello' in Mandarin?"

"Of course!" said Yin. "*Ni hao!*"

"So Turnip Cake has come at last." Yang had appeared from the next room, with his broken foot lifted a few inches off the ground. Instead of hopping, he simply wiggled his good foot, and it slid along the floor.

"You don't need crutches?" said Stanley in amazement. It looked almost like Yang was on a conveyor belt.

"I am a Flying Chinese Wonder,"

answered Yang. "I don't need two feet to walk."

"How do you feel after your trip?" asked Yin.

Stanley wanted to be a polite guest, but he also believed in honesty. "I'm *starving*," he admitted.

Without hesitation, Yin and Yang exchanged looks, tossed coats to each other through the air, and spun Stanley back out the front door.

# Chinese Food

The restaurant was crowded with people, but there was no food on the round tables, apart from a tiny steaming bowl of tea in front of each person. Stanley suddenly realized: Everyone had been waiting for *him*.

There was a hush as the oldest-looking woman Stanley had ever seen— older, even, than Carlos's grandmother

in Mexico—
struggled to
her feet at the
other side of
the room.

Yin whispered in Stanley's ear. "Great Grandmother Yin would like to wish you luck before you begin your training."

Stanley was about to walk over, but Yang stopped him with a hand on his shoulder.

The ancient

woman slowly straightened her back, raised her shaking hands from the back of a chair . . . and launched herself into the air. She flipped onto the nearest table, and then did handsprings from one table to another, all the way around the room. She failed to disturb a single cup of tea before landing right in front of Stanley and giving him a toothless smile.

Stanley was stunned. The old woman giggled, grabbed him by the sides of his stomach, and shook him. He couldn't help laughing as his head and feet swung back and forth through the air . . . and then, suddenly, his body made a low rhythmic sound as the air rushed around him.

Stanley didn't know his body could do that!

Yin and Yang and their family roared with laughter.

Everybody waited to fill their plates until Yin and Yang's grandparents and great grandparents were served. Then, as all of the relatives chattered and slurped and ate, Stanley carefully adjusted his chopsticks and tried to pick up a piece of food.

Instead, one of the chopsticks tilted like a seesaw, and the piece landed in Yang's soup with a splash.

Yang put down his own chopsticks. "It is time for Turnip Cake's first lesson," he announced.

Yin nodded in agreement. "Let's start with an ancient feat of balance and skill!" Stanley leaned closer. "Holding—"

"—A pencil," finished Yang.

Stanley rolled his eyes. "I already know how to do *that*," he said, holding one of his chopsticks like a pencil and moving it up and down.

"You are very skilled," teased Yang.

"Now, do you see the cradle formed by your thumb and first finger?" asked Yin. "That is where the other, sleeping chopstick lies its head. Its leg rests on your fourth finger. Look, it does not move! It only sleeps."

Stanley slipped the second chopstick into its cradle.

Lifting his bowl, Stanley used the first chopstick to trap a piece of food against the one resting below it. He carefully lifted the food to his mouth and dropped it in.

It worked! Stanley immediately tried again.

"Turnip Cake learns fast," Yang commented, as Stanley flung one thing after another into his mouth.

Stanley tried lots of new things—rice with meat cooked in a leaf; spicy pork and vegetables; even turnip cake, which was surprisingly jiggly. But his favorite dish of all was a local specialty: biang biang noodles, which were almost as flat and wide as he was.

As Yin and Yang's aunts, uncles, cousins, grandparents, and great grandparents filed by his table to say good-bye, Stanley was so full, he almost didn't feel flat. He couldn't understand a word anyone said, but they all seemed very friendly. Great Grandmother Yin made music by shaking his sides one more time before hobbling out the door.

Soon, Yin, Yang, and Stanley were the only ones left. It was getting late, and Stanley was tired.

But then, out of nowhere, a squinting old man with three long white hairs sprouting from his chin appeared at the table.

"Hello, young ones," wheezed the man in English. "Hello, Flattened Stanley."

"Hello, Great Uncle Yang," said Yin. "We did not see you."

"I have been hiding behind the teapots," said Great Uncle Yang.

Stanley was speechless. Finally, he forced himself to say, "How do you do?"

"With a great deal of practice," the old man replied. "As you can see, teapots are very small."

"Great Uncle Yang is a contortionist!" explained Yin. "He can twist himself into many unusual positions."

"Your body must be very flexible," marveled Stanley.

"No more flexible than yours," the man said with a smile. "But my mind bends farther."

Stanley's forehead crinkled as he tried to figure out what that meant. He decided to change the subject. "Yang has the same name as you."

Yin laughed. "Many in our family are named Yin and Yang," she explained. "Our ancestors have been known throughout China for centuries."

"It was my sister Yin who greeted you," said the old man.

"Great Grandmother Yin is your sister?!" Stanley gasped.

Great Uncle Yang chuckled to himself. Then he fixed Stanley with a powerful stare. "You cannot have Yin without Yang. Understand?"

Stanley looked at him blankly.

"Yin and Yang are not only our names. They are words that describe the sacred balance of nature! There is no day without night. There is no hot without cold." He looked from Yin—"There is no tempest"—to Yang—"without calm. And there is no flat without—" His voice trailed off suddenly.

"Thick?" Stanley offered.

"Fat," suggested Yin.

"Round," tried Yang.

"Without *not flat*," Great Uncle Yang finished. "*Yin* and *yang* mean 'opposing forces in balance.'

"This, Flattened Stanley, is why you are here," the man said. "*You* keep *them* in balance. There are only ten days left before the Flying Chinese Wonders are to perform in the Forbidden City. All three of you have much to learn and much to teach. Are you ready?"

The three of them nodded.

"Begin with Mount Huashan," said Great Uncle Yang. Then he whisked a napkin from the table, shook it, and disappeared into thin air.

# Learning to Fly

The next day, Stanley pressed his back against the face of Mount Huashan. Slowly, he inched along the narrow walkway.

"Come on!" called Yin from up ahead.

Yang whizzed by Stanley's face doing a one-legged cartwheel. "Let's go, Turnip Cake!"

Stanley made the mistake of looking down. The bottom of the valley was nearly six thousand feet below.

Terrified, he looked up again, only to find that he had come to the end of the walkway. Yin and Yang were nowhere to be seen.

Stanley looked around in a panic. He found the twins overhead, swiftly climbing a thick iron chain that reached up the mountain.

Stanley took a deep breath. With a grunt, he started pulling himself up.

When he reached the top, Stanley flopped facedown on the ground with a slap. He'd finally made it—

"Hey, Stanley!" Yin's voice called.

"Keep moving like that," echoed Yang, "and we'll never get to Beijing."

Stanley peeled himself from the ground. In front of him stretched a staircase carved into the rock.

I promised I'd do my best, thought Stanley. He forced himself to go on.

At last, his whole body aching, Stanley reached the end of the staircase. Before him stood an ancient temple.

Now where are Yin and Yang? he thought.

Suddenly, Yang's upside-down face appeared before his eyes. Yin was dangling her brother by the foot from the roof of the temple.

"You coming?" asked Yang, grabbing

Stanley's hands.

Stanley landed flat on his back on the roof with a thud.

"Ow," Stanley groaned.

Yin and Yang smiled down at him.

"Finally," said Yang.

"We can begin your training at last!" said Yin.

On the temple roof atop one of the five peaks of Mount Huashan, Yin twirled on one foot like a ballerina. With Stanley holding her wrists, she swung his body round and round over her head. He was getting dizzier and dizzier.

He felt sick. His palms were sweaty . . . and then they started to slip.

In an instant Stanley had lost his grip.

"Stanley!" cried Yin, as Stanley soared off the mountain peak. He sensed a gust of wind and arched his back. The wind lifted him, and he did a backflip to land on the roof.

"Ta-da!" he panted.

Yin laughed. "You are crazier than a yak!"

Yang turned down the corners of his mouth. "Again," he said, perched like a stork on his good foot.

With only five days left, Stanley, Yin, and Yang stood in a narrow pit filled with row after row of warriors made of clay. Some were taller than Stanley.

Arthur would love this! he thought.

"This is the Terracotta Army. They were buried with the first emperor of China in 210 B.C.," explained Yin. "Only a few foreigners, like Queen Elizabeth the Second, have been allowed to walk through the pits as you do now. These artifacts are priceless!"

"I'll try not to break any," joked Stanley.

"Good idea," replied Yang without smiling.

Without warning, Yin dived headfirst into the army. She bounced and flipped, springing among the soldiers like a grasshopper. Without toppling a single

one, she landed back beside Stanley.

"Now, Turnip Cake," Yang said.

Stanley's mouth hung open. Yin and Yang raised their eyebrows at him.

He shut his mouth. Shaking his head, Stanley took a deep breath and plunged into the army.

He hit the ground with both hands and pushed back up, landing on his toes. He cartwheeled into a flip and—

His right pinkie toe hit a clay horse. It somersaulted into the air.

Stanley perched his fingers and toes on the heads of two soldiers. He arched his back. The horse bounced off his belly like a trampoline. To his surprise, the horse landed back in its place.

Stanley touched down next to Yin and Yang.

"You have more flow than the Yangtze River!" said Yin.

Stanley beamed.

Yang did not look at him. "Beginner's luck," he pronounced.

The big performance was only three days away. Stanley couldn't believe where they were now: on top of the Great Wall of China!

Of all the places in the world Stanley had always wanted to visit, the Great Wall was at the top of his list. He'd learned in school that it was more than 4,000 miles long. That was more miles than it takes to cross the entire United States of America!

"Let's teach Stanley the Ancient Wheel!" said Yin, as a group of schoolchildren in uniforms flowed past.

Yang shook his head. "He is not ready."

"How hard can it be?" Stanley asked. After all, he'd been training for over a week.

"But, brother," said Yin, "the performance in the Forbidden City is the day after tomorrow!"

"The Ancient Wheel is what injured me," Yang responded. "We cannot afford another accident."

"You mean the human circle?!" cried Stanley, remembering the performance in his school auditorium. "That's my favorite part!"

Yin bit her lip. "My brother is right," she admitted abruptly. "You're not ready."

"What?" Stanley gasped. "Why?"

"The sacred art of balance is difficult to master," said Yang. His broken foot quivered in the air. "It requires wisdom. The Ancient Wheel is not to be taken lightly!"

"I'm sorry," said Stanley. "I just . . . Please let me try."

Yin and Yang exchanged doubtful looks.

Moments later, Stanley hung upside down, holding Yin's feet while she held his. They curved their bodies outward and expanded into a circle.

Together they exhaled, and the Ancient Wheel started to roll.

The stones of the ground rolled up and Stanley shut his eyes. He opened them again to see the sky rise swiftly in his view. Just as quickly, it dipped down and his nose met the ground again.

Darkness, sky, ground. Darkness, sky, ground. Faster and faster and faster.

"Slow down!" Yin's voice sounded from far away.

Somebody screamed, and Stanley

glimpsed a flurry of black shoes. They were about to barrel into the schoolchildren!

Stanley stuck out a foot in an attempt to stop. Instead, he lurched over the edge of the Great Wall. Their circle came undone. Stanley felt himself falling, but then Yin grabbed his foot and pulled hard. Miraculously, they landed again on the edge of the wall.

"You must be luckier than the number eight," panted Yin.

All the schoolchildren in their black shoes cheered, as if Stanley and Yin had meant to do all this on purpose. Their teacher, however, frowned at Stanley and Yin, and swiftly corralled the children away.

Stanley waved sheepishly to Yang, who was standing back where the Wheel had begun, but Yang did not wave back. Instead, he bowed his head sadly and turned away.

# To Beijing

Stanley and Yin finally found Yang high up in the branches of a tree.

They called to him, but he would not answer.

Stanley leaned his chest against the trunk, and Yin bounced off his back and up into the branches. She hung upside down from her knees and pulled him up after her.

They perched silently on a thick branch on either side of Yang. Eventually he spoke.

"The great balance of Yin and Yang is off," he said. "I know you want to help, Turnip Cake. But there are only two of us: Yin and Yang. Night and day. Hot and cold. Opposing forces in balance."

"But it's my job to keep you in balance!" said Stanley. "That's what Great Uncle Yang said!"

"How?" wondered Yang. "By showing off and being careless? By putting schoolchildren in danger?"

Stanley sighed. Yang was right: Stanley was just a third wheel. He'd never be as good as them.

"I was trying to prove I could do it." Stanley pouted.

"You do not understand," said Yin gently. "Forget what you can do. Forget everything. When you stop *trying* . . ."

"That is when you will be ready," finished Yang.

All that day and through the next, Stanley practiced with Yin and Yang. He learned the Flying Monkey. He mastered the Leaping Fish. He was fitted for a Flying Wonders costume.

And then it was time to go.

They arrived in Beijing on the morning of the big performance. It was only there that Stanley realized how famous Yin and Yang were. They rode in a limousine, which was led through the streets by police cars. Yin and Yang rolled down the windows and waved to the crowds.

Nearly every shop and building was hung with red decorations to celebrate the Chinese New Year, and the sidewalks were full of children carrying red lanterns shaped like birds, dragons, and butterflies. Yin explained that tonight was the Lantern Festival, the culmination of the New Year celebrations. It was for this occasion that the Flying Chinese Wonders had been invited to perform within the Forbidden City in the center of Beijing.

"Is the city really forbidden?" Stanley asked.

"Not anymore," said Yang.

"Now anyone can go to the Palace Museum," continued Yin. "But for five hundred years, the Imperial Palace had been home to Chinese emperors!"

The limousine stopped and a police officer opened the door. Stanley climbed out after Yin and Yang. A short man in glasses pumped their hands enthusiastically.

"This is the mayor of Beijing!" Yin explained. "He wants to give us a special tour of the zoo."

Stanley had seen a lot of animals up

close when he was in Africa, but this was by far the best zoo he'd been to. He saw tiny golden snub-nosed monkeys, which lived only in China. He saw Manchurian tigers—tigers didn't exist naturally in Africa. He even saw a sea turtle bigger than the bulletin board that flattened him.

And then Stanley saw the giant pandas. They stared out from their enclosure with their big, friendly black eyes on either side of their furry white faces.

"My mom loves giant pandas!" said Stanley. "Can one of you take a picture of me in front of them?"

Yang held up the camera and

frowned. "I wish you could get closer."

The mayor and police officers had moved on down the path. Without saying another word, Yang looked meaningfully at Stanley as Yin gestured silently to his feet.

Stanley looked down and saw that the fence surrounding the pandas stopped less than an inch above the ground. His eyes widened.

Yin and Yang nodded quickly.

Without a word, Stanley slid under the fence and popped up on the other side.

He smiled his biggest smile for the camera.

A growl rose up behind him.

The camera flashed. A searing pain tore down Stanley's right side.

Stanley looked down . . . and then he passed out.

# The Lucky One

Stanley opened his eyes.

He saw a diagram of a body on the wall and realized that he was lying in some kind of doctor's office. A man in a white coat appeared above him, flanked by Yin and Yang.

"I am Doctor Don," said the man.

"Doctor Dan?" said Stanley.

"Doctor *Don*," repeated the man, as

he fiddled with something at the other end of the table.

Stanley felt a small pinch in his foot. At once, the pain in his side disappeared.

He tucked his chin so he could see what Doctor Don was doing.

Stanley gasped. There was a quivering needle as thin as a thread sticking right through his flat foot!

"Chinese acupuncture," explained Doctor Don. "It is very good for the relief of pain."

"How does it work?" asked Stanley.

Doctor Don smiled. "Sometimes we doctors can only marvel at how little we really know."

Stanley blinked. He was sure Doctor

Dan had said almost the exact same thing after Stanley was flattened!

"What happened to me?" Stanley asked.

"It was the panda," Yin said. Yang held up the photograph. There was Stanley, smiling broadly as a big white furry face with black eyes lunged ferociously behind him.

Stanley sat up and peeled back the bandage that stretched along the right side of his stomach. Close to his edge, he found a tear a few inches long.

He could see right through himself.

I'm hurt! Stanley thought in shock. This was the first time he had been hurt since becoming flat. He'd always

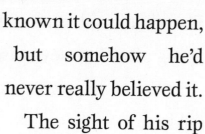

known it could happen, but somehow he'd never really believed it. The sight of his rip was making Stanley dizzy, so he lay back down.

"You are very lucky," said Doctor Don. "There was almost no blood."

Suddenly, Stanley jumped up again. He remembered what day it was.

"The performance!" he cried. "What time is it?"

"We have to be in the Forbidden City soon," replied Yin.

"I can do it," Stanley said in a brave voice.

"I don't think that would be wise," cautioned Doctor Don.

"But it doesn't hurt anymore!" said Stanley.

Yang shook his head. "The tear has changed the shape of your body, Turnip Cake. Air will not flow around you in the same way."

"But . . . what will you do?"

Yang took a deep breath. "Confucius said, 'Our greatest glory is not in never failing, but in getting up every time we do.'"

With that, Yang lowered his broken foot and walked carefully across the room. Gaining speed, he walked up the wall and backflipped to the ground.

"Brother, you are healed!" cried Yin.

Doctor Don bent down and wiggled Yang's foot. "Remarkable," he murmured.

Stanley felt like a heavy rock was falling deep inside his stomach.

"You don't need me," he said in a soft voice. He tried to smile. "I'm sure you two will be great."

# In Balance

"Mom?" Stanley said into the phone.

"Stanley, is that you?" Harriet Lambchop's voice nearly leaped through the receiver. "Oh, how we miss you! How's China?"

Stanley couldn't speak.

"What is it, dear? Is everything all right?"

"I got hurt," Stanley blurted. All at

once, he started to cry.

Mr. Lambchop picked up the other extension. "Now calm down, Stanley. I'm sure you're all right. What happened?"

"I bot born by a banda bear," blubbered Stanley.

"A panda bear?" gasped his mother.

"Uh huh," replied Stanley.

"But they're so adorable!" said Harriet Lambchop.

Stanley tried to catch his breath long enough to get the next part out. "It was really scary. I got a rip from its claw. You can see right through me."

There was a loud thump on the other end of the phone.

"Hello?" said Stanley.

"Stanley, talk to your brother for a moment," said Mr. Lambchop. "I think your mother just fainted."

Arthur got on the line. "What's up, bro?"

"Hi, Arthur."

"When's the big show?"

"In an hour," sighed Stanley. "But I can't be in it."

"Why not?"

"Because I got hurt! I worked so hard, Arthur. I climbed a mountain and bounced through an army and rolled on the Great Wall. I finally mastered a Double Flying Dragon. But now I won't get to do any of it!"

"Slow down," said Arthur. "I didn't understand half of what you just said. Start from the beginning, and tell me everything."

Stanley did. He told Arthur about the twins' Great Grandmother Yin and Great Uncle Yang, and the meaning of Yin and Yang, and how he learned to use chopsticks. He told him about climbing Mount Huashan and practicing on the roof of the temple, and about when they trained among the Terracotta Army soldiers, which Arthur thought was terrific, just like Stanley thought he would. He told him about the accident on the Great Wall and how Yang responded, and the two days of intense practice that followed. He told him about Beijing, and the limousine, and the zoo, and the panda, and the picture, and Doctor Don who was just like Doctor Dan, and Yang's miraculous recovery, and how now he was all alone calling home and feeling sorry for himself.

Arthur didn't say anything for a long time.

Then he said, "Have you tried duct tape?"

"What do you mean have I tried—" Stanley froze. He lifted up his shirt and peered at his wound.

"Arthur," Stanley cried, "you're a genius!"

*　*　*

In the center of Beijing, in the heart of the Forbidden City, Stanley stood nervously between Yin and Yang as a giant red velvet curtain parted before their eyes. A wave of rapturous applause rushed over them.

They bowed slowly. In a balcony, the president of China nodded and smiled.

And then, together, the three Flying Wonders shot into the air.

Stanley felt the rushing air on his skin, and the grasp of the twins' hands, and the light rubbery bounce of his toes touching down and springing back up. He felt the top of his head brush the back of his ankles. At times, he could not tell

where his body ended and theirs began.

A giant flaming torch rose up in the center of the stage, and Yin and Yang encircled it and stretched Stanley before the audience. He felt the heat on his back as the light glowed through his thinning body: a human Chinese New Year's lantern. The crowd went wild.

Yin turned upside down beside Stanley. He faced her back, while Yang faced his. The twins curved their bodies outward, the three of them exhaled deeply, and the Wheel started to turn. It rolled majestically around the stage, with Stanley's flat body forming an S through its center.

They were the essence of the ancient

symbol of Yin and Yang: opposing forces in balance.

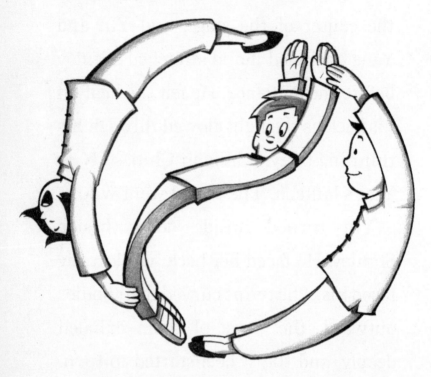

The audience rose to their feet. In the front row, Great Grandmother Yin and Great Uncle Yang cheered loudest of all.

# Small Wonders

Arthur crouched on top of the bookshelf in the corner of the room he and Stanley shared. "Ready?" he asked.

"Ready," said Stanley. "Remember, don't—"

Arthur leaped from the bookshelf and belly-flopped onto the bed. He bounced up into the air . . . waved his arms and legs . . . and crashed right into

Stanley, flattening him to the ground.

Mr. Lambchop appeared in the doorway. "Arthur," he asked, "don't you think your brother is flat enough already?"

Arthur got up off Stanley. "Stanley's training me!" he said excitedly.

"That was *not* what I told you to do," said Stanley.

"Was too!" said Arthur.

"Was not!"

"Was too!"

"Was not!"

"I understand." Mr. Lambchop nodded wisely. "You are opposing forces in balance."

"Boys!" called Mrs. Lambchop.

"Your friend Carlos is here!"

Carlos bounded into the room. "Stanley, you are back!" he said. "How was China?"

"Amazing," Stanley replied. "I got torn by a giant panda bear."

"No!" Carlos's eyes bulged.

Arthur gestured to the bulletin board, where Stanley had hung the photograph that Yang had taken at the zoo. Carlos took one look

and let out a long whistle.

"Stanley was just training me to be a Flying Wonder," announced Arthur.

"Oh," said Carlos. "I can come back later."

Stanley looked at him curiously.

"You need only two people to play Flying Chinese Wonders," Carlos explained with a frown. "I do not want to be a third wheel."

Stanley smiled. "You don't understand," he said gently. He positioned Arthur on one side of the room, and Carlos on the other. "Sometimes, for balance," he continued, climbing atop the bed, "a third wheel is just what you need."

And with that, Stanley Lambchop
shot into the air.

# In his worldwide adventures so far, Flat Stanley has:

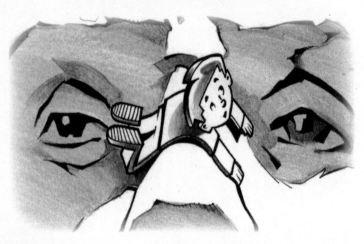

Stopped Mount Rushmore from collapsing!

Rescued the priceless Egyptian Giant Scrolls of Papyrus!

Battled with deadly ninjas in Japan!

Competed in the Olympics in Canada—
as a human snowboard!

Helped a famous matador in a Mexican bullfight!

And he's canoed down an African river!

Don't miss Flat Stanley's next two
worldwide adventures...

*The Australian Boomerang Bonanza*
and
*The US Capital Commotion!*

Flat Stanley's Worldwide Adventures #1:
# THE MOUNT RUSHMORE CALAMITY

Flat Stanley's Worldwide Adventures #2:
# THE GREAT EGYPTIAN GRAVE ROBBERY

Flat Stanley's Worldwide Adventures #3:
# THE JAPANESE NINJA SURPRISE

Flat Stanley's Worldwide Adventures #4:
# THE INTREPID CANADIAN EXPEDITION

Flat Stanley's Worldwide Adventures #5:
# THE AMAZING MEXICAN SECRET

Flat Stanley's Worldwide Adventures #6:
# THE AFRICAN SAFARI DISCOVERY